Animal Stories
... with Picture Clues!

Copyright © 2012 Highlights for Children, Inc.
All rights reserved.

Published by Highlights for Children, Inc.
P.O. Box 18201
Columbus, Ohio 43218-0201
Printed in USA

ISBN 1-62091-004-7

First edition, 2012

www.Highlights.com

A Day at the Pond

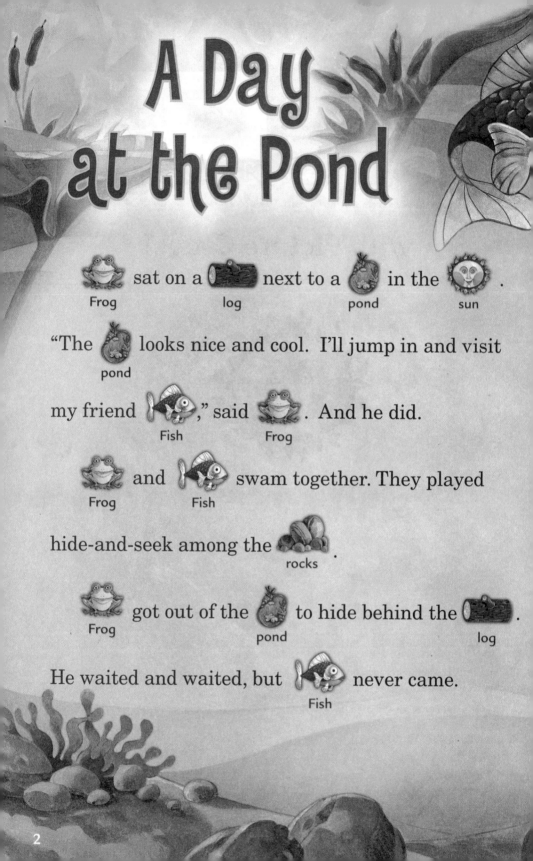

Frog sat on a log next to a pond in the sun.

"The pond looks nice and cool. I'll jump in and visit my friend Fish," said Frog. And he did.

Frog and Fish swam together. They played hide-and-seek among the rocks.

Frog got out of the pond to hide behind the log.

He waited and waited, but Fish never came.

So he jumped back into

the 🟤 . "Where were you?"
pond

🐸 asked 🐟 . "You
Frog   Fish

never found me."

"I can't leave the 🟤 ," said 🐟 .
pond   Fish

"You hid where I *can't* find you!"

Story by Linda Paterson • Art by David Galchutt

Bear Rides!

Bear and Dad walked

to the **fair** . Bear said,

"Look, a **merry-go-round** ! Can we

please ride on it?"

"Sure," said Dad. Bear and Dad rode

on **2** **two** horses **horses** .

Dad pointed to a **train** . "Let's hop on." The

train puffed along the **tracks** . Bear and

Dad rode in the **caboose** .

After that, they rode in a **spaceship** .

The  slid down.

sun

"We should head home now," said Dad.

Bear began to walk, but his felt tired.

legs

"I think it's time for another ride," said Dad.

So Bear rode to the on Dad's !

house   shoulders

Story by Maggie Murphy • Art by Robert Squier

Cock-a-Doodle Doo!

 watched the ☺ rise. He yawned.

Rooster · sun

"I'm tired of crowing. I want to do something else."

He marched into the 🏠 . "Wake up!" he called.

barn

"Someone must greet the ☺ ."

sun

"I'll greet the ☺ ," said 🐓 . "But you

sun · Hen

must lay 🥚 ."

eggs

"I'll greet the ☺ ," said 🐄 .

sun · Cow

"But you must give  ."

milk

"I'll greet the ☺ ," said 🐑 . "But you

sun   Sheep

must give 🌾 ."

wool

🐓 couldn't lay 🥚 or give 🪣 .

Rooster   eggs   milk

He didn't have any 🌾 . But he could crow!

wool

"Thanks, friends," said 🐓 . "I will greet the ☺ ."

Rooster   sun

Story by Lynne Marie Pisano and Connie Marie Cheney • Art by Bill Dickson

A Horse to Love

I ride the  to ___ each day.
bus   school

I pass the same ___ on my way.
horse

At times he's outdoors eating ___
grass

beside a rail ___ when I pass.
fence

The ___ is spotted ___ on ___ .
horse   gray   white

His ___ and ___ and ___ are light.
ears   mane   tail

I'd like to take the ___ a treat,
horse

a ___ or some ___ to eat.
carrot   fruit

I'd like to pat his
ears

and  ,
nose

and rub his  .
neck

Do you suppose

I'll have a
horse

when I am grown?

A spotted
horse

to love? My own?

Story by Pat Lessie • Art by Bonnie Leick

Music in the Dark

 plays his  . *Brreeet! BRUP!*

Mosquito   trumpet

"Wrong  ,  ," chirps  .

note   Mosquito   Cricket

 plays his  . *Plinkity PLUNK!*

Cricket   violin

"You're both wrong!" squeals  .

Beetle

 plays her  . *Zzzum! ZAT!*

Beetle   bass

"Still wrong,"  and  say.

Cricket   Mosquito

Story by Michelle Benjamin • Art by Bonnie Leick

They play together. *BRUP! PLUNK! ZAT!*

"Where is 🪰 ?" cry 🦗 and 🦟

Firefly **Cricket** **Mosquito**

and 🪲 . "Sorry I'm late!" 🪰 says,

Beetle **Firefly**

landing on their 🍃. 🪰 glows.

leaf **Firefly**

The sheet music shows. "Now

we know the right 🎵 to

notes

play!" say 🦗 and 🦟

Cricket **Mosquito**

and 🪲 . They *BRREEET!*

Beetle

and *PLINK!* and *ZZZUM!* until the

 comes up.

sun

A **Big** Dinner for **Little** Mouse

Mama Mouse put dinner on the [table] for Little
Mouse. She put out [milk], [carrots], [fish], and [peanuts].

As Little Mouse ate, he talked to Mama Mouse.

"If I drink my [milk], I'll be as strong as an [ox].

If I eat my [carrots], I'll be as fast as a [rabbit]. If I
eat my [fish], I'll be sharp-eyed like an [owl].

If I eat my  , I'll have the good memory of an

peanuts

." By the time Little Mouse had finished

elephant

eating, the was high in the sky.

moon

"It's time for ," said Mama Mouse. She

bed

tucked Little Mouse into and said,

bed

"Now it's time for you to be as

quiet as a ."

mouse

Story by Ruth Schiffmann • Art by Valerie Sokolova

The Home-Grown Gifts

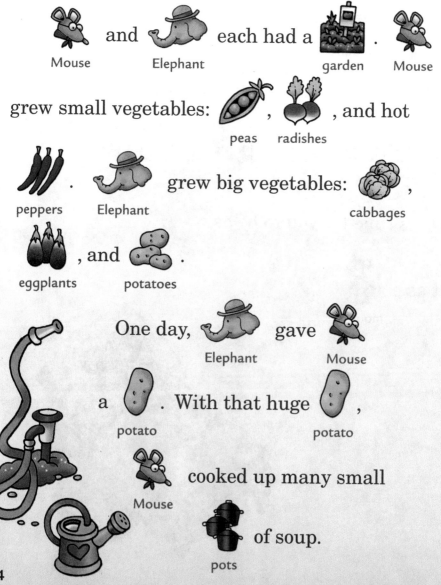

Mouse and Elephant each had a garden. Mouse grew small vegetables: peas, radishes, and hot peppers. Elephant grew big vegetables: cabbages, eggplants, and potatoes.

One day, Elephant gave Mouse a potato. With that huge potato, Mouse cooked up many small pots of soup.

 Mouse thought, "I want to thank  Elephant

with a gift from *my*  garden . But my  radishes

and  peas are too small.  Elephant could eat them

all in one bite."

Then  Mouse had an idea. He gave his friend

a  basket of hot  peppers . With those tiny hot

 peppers ,  Elephant cooked up a big  pot

of spicy chili!

Story by Maggie Murphy • Art by R. Michael Palan

Crow Gets a Drink

Based on a fable by Aesop

The 🌊 was dry. The ☀️ grew hotter.
stream   sun

🐦 was thirsty for some water.
Crow

With her sharp 👁 👁, 🐦 could see
eyes   Crow

a 🫙 of water near a 🌳.
jug   tree

🐦 flew down to the 🌳 to check.
Crow   tree

The glass 🫙 had a narrow 🫙.
jug   neck

The water was not high inside.

🐦 couldn't reach it when she tried.
Crow

How could 🐦 make the water rise?
Crow

She found some 🪨 just the right size.
pebbles

Story by Pat Lessie • Art by Meryl Henderson

She dropped them in

the , and each

jug

helped raise the water

so could reach.

Crow

She filled her

beak

and drank until

her thirst was gone.

 had her fill.

Crow

The Strongest Animal in the Jungle

"I am the strongest animal in the 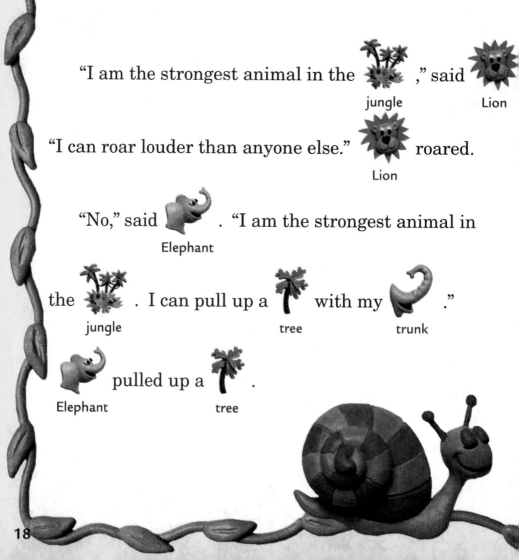 ," said

jungle

Lion

"I can roar louder than anyone else." Lion roared.

"No," said Elephant. "I am the strongest animal in

the jungle. I can pull up a tree with my trunk."

Elephant pulled up a tree.

18

Story by Susan Taylor • Art by Amy Vansgard

Then **Snail** spoke up. "**Lion**, you are not the strongest animal. **Elephant**, you are not the strongest animal. *I* am the strongest animal," said **Snail**.

Lion and **Elephant** laughed. "What makes you so strong, **Snail**?" they asked.

"I can carry my **house** on my back," said **Snail**. And he did.

Good Morning, Good Night!

Robin hopped out of her nest early one

morning before the sun came up. Owl was

still awake. "I love the sunrise," sang Robin.

"I love the sunset," hooted Owl. He yawned

and fluffed his feathers.

Robin stretched her wings. "I love the sun,"

said Robin.

Owl said, "The moon is better."

"Just give the sun

a chance," chirped Robin.

"Well, I'll try," said

Owl. He blinked

his tired eyes.

Up came the sun. "Isn't it amazing?"

asked Robin.

"Zzzz," said Owl.

Story by Maggie Murphy • Art by Jamison Odone

The FOX and the Crow

Based on a fable by Aesop

A  found a piece of and flew up
crow   cheese

into a tall . But before the could eat
tree   crow

the , a hungry came by.
cheese   fox

"My!" said the slyly. "What a fine
fox

you are! Your shine
crow   feathers

like the . Your
sun   wings

are stronger than

the ."
wind

22

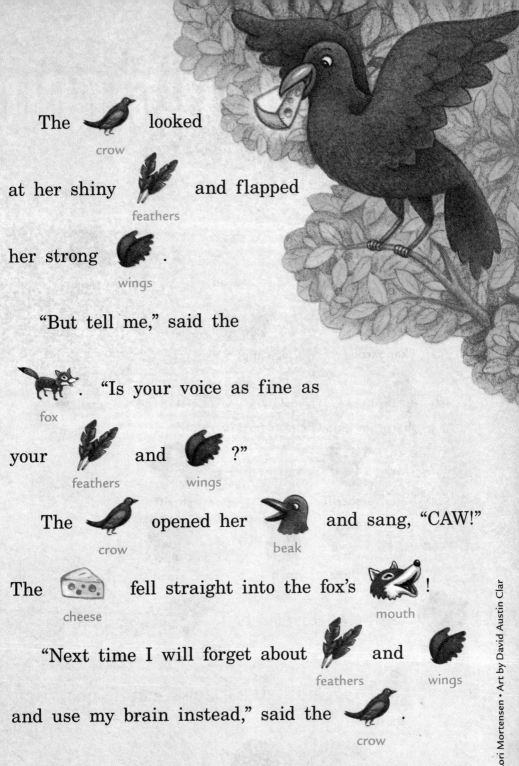

The looked
crow

at her shiny feathers and flapped

her strong wings.

"But tell me," said the

fox. "Is your voice as fine as

your feathers and wings?"

The crow opened her beak and sang, "CAW!"

The cheese fell straight into the fox's mouth!

"Next time I will forget about feathers and

and use my brain instead," said the crow.

Story by Lori Mortensen • Art by David Austin Clar

A Cold Kangaroo

Based on a real-life event in southern Wisconsin

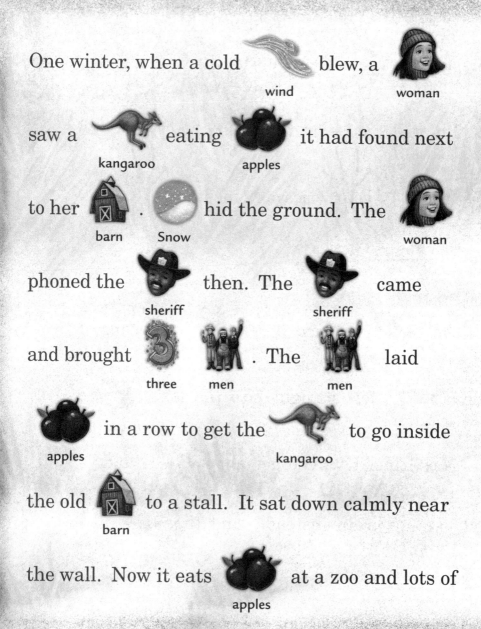

One winter, when a cold **wind** blew, a **woman** saw a **kangaroo** eating **apples** it had found next to her **barn**. **Snow** hid the ground. The **woman** phoned the **sheriff** then. The **sheriff** came and brought **three men**. The **men** laid **apples** in a row to get the **kangaroo** to go inside the old **barn** to a stall. It sat down calmly near the wall. Now it eats **apples** at a zoo and lots of

, too. Why was it hopping through cold

sweet potatoes

in winter ? We still don't know.

snow   wind

Story by Pat Lessie • Art by John Shroades

25

Flowers for Mouse

One morning,  Squirrel called, " Mouse , come out

and smell the flowers ."

"I can't," said Mouse . " Flowers make my

nose itch."

Later, Raccoon knocked on Mouse's door. He held

a jar of flowers . "Look at the beautiful flowers ,

Mouse ," said Raccoon .

"I can't," said Mouse . " Flowers

make my eyes water."

That evening,  and **Raccoon** brought **Mouse**

a surprise. "This **cake** is for you," **Squirrel** said.

The **cake** was covered with **flowers** made

of icing.

"Thank you!" said **Mouse** . "These **flowers** are

just right for me."

Story by Katy S. Duffield • Art by Karen Loccisano and R. Michael Palan

Ostrich Takes Off

"I want to fly," said  .

Ostrich

"Why don't you spread your wings ?"

asked Warthog .

Ostrich spread her wings .

"You're not flying," said Giraffe .

"Why don't you flap your wings ?"

Ostrich flapped her wings .

"You're still not flying," said  . "Why

Zebra

don't you run and flap your  ?"

wings

 ran and flapped her  .

Ostrich   wings

"You're still not flying,

but you're one fast runner!"

said  .

Elephant

"Thank you," said  .

Ostrich

Story by Jessica Lee Anderson • Art by Christopher R. Mills

Buddy wanted a new 🏠 . First he had

to sell his old one. He put up a sign: 🏠 for sale.

But no 🐕🐕🐕 wanted to buy it.

So Buddy painted his 🏠 🟦 . He put

up a new sign: 🟦 🏠 for sale.

No 🐕🐕🐕 came by.

Then Buddy added new 🪟 and

a new 🏠 . He put up a new sign: 🟦

30

 with new  and a new  for sale.

doghouse   windows   roof

Still no  came by.

dogs

Next Buddy put in a  with a  .

pool   fence

He planted  and a  . He smiled when

flowers   tree

he looked at his  .

doghouse

Now lots of  were interested!

dogs

"It's not for sale," Buddy said as he took down

the sign. Then he put on his  and took a dip.

bathing suit

Story by Kathleen Doherty • Art by David Helton

A Tale of Two Mice

Based on a fable by Aesop

One day Country 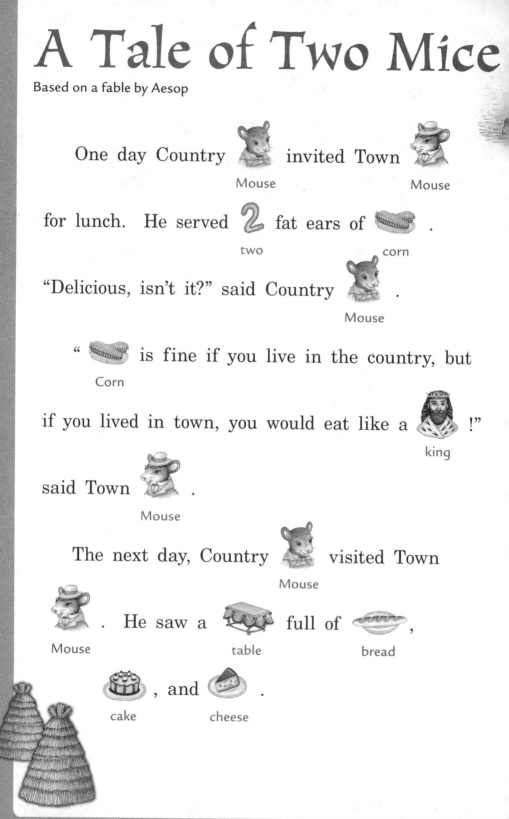 invited Town
Mouse   Mouse

for lunch. He served 2 fat ears of corn.
two   corn

"Delicious, isn't it?" said Country
Mouse.

" Corn is fine if you live in the country, but
Corn

if you lived in town, you would eat like a king !"
king

said Town
Mouse.

The next day, Country visited Town
Mouse

Mouse. He saw a table full of bread,
table   bread

cake, and cheese.
cake   cheese

"You are right," said Country .
Mouse

"You do eat like a  !"
king

But before Country  could take a bite,
Mouse

 chased the  away. "Good-bye!" said
Dog   mice

Country . "You eat like a , but
Mouse   king

you must run from . At home I can
Dog

eat  in peace."
corn

Story by Lori Mortensen • Art by Valerie Sokolova

April Fool for Mo and Joe

It was April Fools' Day.

Mo wanted to play a trick

on Joe. "I know," said Mo. "I'll turn the milk yellow."

Mo squeezed **8** eight drops of yellow food coloring

into the milk. He closed the carton and shook it **9** nine

times. He left the room.

Joe came into the kitchen. He wanted to trick

Mo. "I know," said Joe. "I'll turn the milk blue."

He squeezed **8** eight drops of  blue food coloring into the milk. He closed the carton and shook it **9** nine times.

At breakfast time, Mo poured milk on his cereal. Joe poured milk on his cereal.

" Green milk?" said Mo.

" Green milk?" said Joe.

"I guess the milk played an April Fools' trick on us," they said.

Story by Wendi Silvano • Art by Rocky Fuller

35

One Mitten

Sophie showed Grace an old 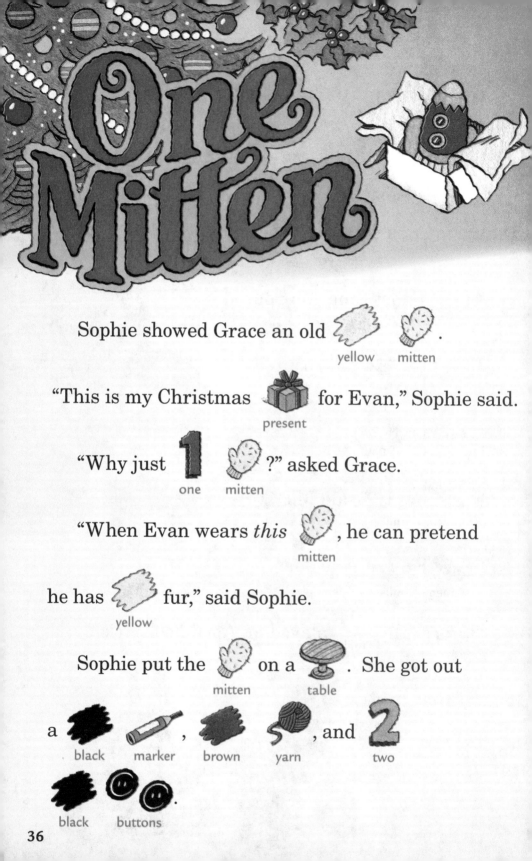 yellow mitten .

"This is my Christmas present for Evan," Sophie said.

"Why just **1** one mitten ?" asked Grace.

"When Evan wears *this* mitten , he can pretend

he has yellow fur," said Sophie.

Sophie put the mitten on a table . She got out

a black marker , brown yarn , and **2** two

black buttons .

The old soon
mitten

became something new.

The next morning, Evan ran

to the 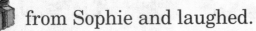. He opened his
Christmas tree

 from Sophie and laughed.
present

"Wow, a 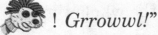! *Grrrowwl!*"
lion puppet

Story by Maggie Murphy • Art by David Helton

The Dog Won't Eat

"I wonder why Fergus didn't eat his dog food," said Tina.

"Look, his bowl is still full."

"I wish I knew," Jack said. "I gave the horses their hay. I put corn out for the chickens and ducks.

I fed the pigs, sheep, goats, cows, and rabbits. Fergus followed me around the whole time."

38

"Now I see why  didn't eat his ,"

Fergus

dog food

 said. She pointed to the . "You left

Tina

door

him outside."

 opened the kitchen .  ran

Jack

door

Fergus

in and ate all of his  in  gulps!

dog food

two

Story by Angela L. Fox • Art by Erin Mauterer

A Good Trade

Sister Bear found a new recipe for honey cakes . "It

makes 6 six honey cakes ," she told Brother Bear . "3 Three for

you and 3 three for me. We need butter , honey ,

flour , and 1 one egg ."

"But we're out of eggs ," said Brother Bear .

40

Sister Bear had an idea. Soon she came

back carrying **one** **egg**.

"Where did you get that?" asked **Brother Bear**.

"I asked **Mrs. Rabbit** to trade **one** **egg**

for **two** **honey cakes**," said **Sister Bear**.

"Now we can make the recipe," **Brother Bear** said.

"**Two** **honey cakes** for you, **two** for me—"

"And **two** for **Mrs. Rabbit**!" said **Sister Bear**.

Story by Heather Tomasello • Art by Valerie Sokolova

Jelly Beans

"Where are you going,  Rabbit ?" asked Turtle .

"To Duck's store ," said Rabbit . "Duck is

having a contest. The one who guesses how many jelly beans

are in a jar is the winner."

"I'll go with you," said Turtle . At Duck's store they

saw a jar of jelly beans . Everyone guessed how many

jelly beans were in the jar .

"Turtle is the winner," said Duck . He handed

Turtle the prize—a gold watch .

 began to cry.

Turtle

"Why are you crying?"  asked.

Rabbit

"You won a  !"

watch

"I didn't want a  ," said  .

watch　　　　　Turtle

"I wanted the  ."

jelly beans

Moose's Birthday

Moose had a birthday. His best friend, Goose,

said, "I'll give Moose a birthday party." She invited

Opossum, Rabbit, Beaver, and Squirrel.

Opossum gave Moose an acorn from the woods.

Moose ate it.

Rabbit gave Moose a purple flower from

Mrs. Callahan's garden. Moose ate it.

44

 gave
Beaver   Moose

a juicy green  from the  .  ate it.
              leaf   pond   Moose

 gave  a big red  from
Squirrel   Moose   apple

Mrs. Callahan's  .  ate it.
                 apple tree   Moose

 gave  a long blue  she had
Goose   Moose   scarf

knitted.  ate it.
          Moose

Story by Bonnie Highsmith Taylor • Art by Kathi Ember

Little Lost Bear

 chased a butterfly through the woods. He

came to a strange pond. "Where am I?" he cried.

"Are you lost?" asked Frog.

"Yes," Bear said. "I can't find my scratching

tree. I can't find my cave. I can't

find Mama Bear."

"I'll help," said Frog. Frog and Bear went

back the way Bear had come. After a while,

 asked, "What are you looking for?"

Frog

 pointed. "For a scratching

Bear

tree

just like this. And a  just like that. With

cave

a  just like her!"  ran to  .

Mama Bear

Bear

Mama Bear

"My little lost  !" cried  .

Bear

Mama Bear

"Thanks to  , I'm little found  !"

Frog

Bear

said  .

Bear

Story by Lynne Marie Pisano • Art by Ron Lieser

Zebra and Lion

Zebra always lost his glasses. Zebra needed his glasses to read the newspaper. Lion found them in a chair. Zebra needed his glasses to read a letter. Lion found them on the table. Zebra needed his glasses to read a book. Lion found them on the desk. "How can I thank you?" asked Zebra.

"You can teach me to read," said Lion.

And Zebra did!